Exploring Linguistics From the Origins of Language to Modern Theories and Applications

A Comprehensive Guide to the Fascinating Study of Human Language

Jonathan Johtdon

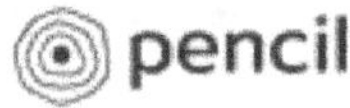

ISBN 978-93-5667-760-9
© Jonathan Johtdon 2023

Published in India 2023 by Pencil

A brand of
One Point Six Technologies Pvt. Ltd.
Unit no. 26, Ground Floor, Building A1,
Wadala Truck Terminal Road,
Near Post Office, Antop Hill, Mumbai - 400037
E connect@thepencilapp.com
W www.thepencilapp.com

DISCLAIMER: *The opinions expressed in this book are those of the authors and do not purport to reflect the views of the Publisher.*

Author biography

Exploring Linguistics From the Origins of Language to Modern Theories and Applications is a comprehensive and accessible book that provides an overview of the study of linguistics. The author of this book is Writer Jonathan Johtdon, a renowned linguist who has made significant contributions to the field of linguistics.Work continues to inspire new generations of linguists around the world.

CONTENTS

Introduction

The Study of Language in Colonial Contexts
Comparative Linguistics and Language Reconstruction
Linguistic Anthropology

Chapter 9: Conclusion

Summary of the Book
Future Directions in Linguistics Research
Implications of Linguistic Knowledge for Society and
Culture.

Chapter 5 History of Linguistic Doctrines - From Aristotle to Contrastive Linguistics

The study of linguistics has a long and fascinating history, with many different approaches and theories emerging over time. Aristotle's work laid the groundwork for the systematic study of language, while medieval scholars saw language as a reflection of the divine order of the universe. The Enlightenment brought a focus on empirical observation and scientific method, paving the way for the development of historical linguistics. In the early 20th century, structural linguistics emerged, emphasizing the structure of language over its meaning. Generative linguistics, which developed in the 1950s, focused on the innate capacity of the human mind for language acquisition. Contrastive linguistics, a relatively recent development, seeks to understand the similarities and differences between languages and how they affect language learning and translation.

The history of linguistic doctrines is marked by both continuity and change. Each new approach builds on the work of previous scholars, while also introducing new perspectives and insights. The study of linguistics has expanded and diversified over time, with many different subfields and areas of specialization emerging. Today, linguistics is a vibrant and dynamic field, with ongoing research and debate about the nature of language, its role in human cognition and culture, and its relationship to other areas of study.

One of the key themes that runs throughout the history of linguistic doctrines is the idea of language as a complex and multifaceted phenomenon. Linguistics has always been concerned with understanding the many different aspects of language, from its sound system and grammatical structure to its cultural and social functions. Over time, linguists have developed a range of different tools and techniques for studying language, from descriptive analysis and historical reconstruction to experimental studies and computational modeling.

Another important theme in the history of linguistic doctrines is the relationship between language and the human mind. From Aristotle's belief that language reflects the structure of reality to Chomsky's idea of an innate language faculty, linguists have long been fascinated by the ways in which language is processed and produced by the human brain. This interest has led to the development of fields such as psycholinguistics, which explores the cognitive mechanisms underlying language use, and neurolinguistics, which uses brain imaging techniques to study the neural basis of language processing.

Throughout its history, linguistics has also been shaped by broader social, cultural, and political contexts. The rise of structuralism in the early 20th century, for example, was influenced by the broader intellectual climate of the time, which emphasized the importance of formal analysis and system building. Similarly, the emergence of contrastive linguistics in the post-World War II period was driven in part by the need to understand the linguistic differences between different cultures and nations.

Today, linguistics continues to be an exciting and rapidly evolving field of study. Advances in technology and computing have opened up new possibilities for research and analysis, while increasing globalization and cultural exchange have made the study of language more important than ever. From understanding the complexities of bilingualism and language contact to developing new methods for language teaching and learning, linguistics is a field that has much to offer to our understanding of human language and communication.

In addition to these themes, linguistics has also been concerned with the diversity of languages and the importance of preserving linguistic heritage. With the loss of many indigenous languages and dialects worldwide, linguists have become increasingly interested in documenting and preserving endangered languages. This has led to the development of fields such as language documentation and revitalization, which seek to support language communities in maintaining and revitalizing their languages.

Furthermore, linguistics has also played an important role in shaping language policy and planning. In many countries, language has been a contentious issue, with debates over the status and use of different languages in education, government, and public life. Linguists have been involved in these debates, offering insights into the social and cultural functions of language and advocating for the recognition and support of linguistic diversity.

In recent years, linguistics has also been at the forefront of interdisciplinary research, engaging with fields such as anthropology, sociology, psychology, computer science, and neuroscience. This cross-disciplinary approach has led to new insights into the complex relationships between language, culture, and cognition, and has opened up exciting new avenues for research and collaboration.

Overall, the study of linguistics has a rich and fascinating history, marked by diverse approaches and themes. Today, linguistics continues to be a dynamic and important field, with many opportunities for further exploration and discovery.

Linguistics has been a field of study that has evolved over time to become increasingly interdisciplinary. As linguists have sought to understand the complex nature of language and its role in human cognition, culture, and society, they have turned to a range of different fields and approaches.

One important area of interdisciplinary research in linguistics has been the study of language and cognition. Researchers in this area explore the ways in which language is processed and represented in the brain, and how this relates to other cognitive functions such as memory and attention. They also investigate the role of language in shaping thought and perception, and how different languages and cultural contexts can influence cognitive processes.

Another area of interdisciplinary research in linguistics is the study of language and society. Sociolinguists investigate the social and cultural factors that shape language use, including issues such as language variation and change, multilingualism, and language attitudes and ideologies. Anthropological linguistics, on the other hand, looks at the role of language in shaping culture and society, including the ways in which language is used in rituals, myths, and other cultural practices.

Computational linguistics is another interdisciplinary field that has emerged in recent years, combining the study of language with computer science and artificial intelligence. Researchers in this area develop algorithms and computational models to analyze and process language data, with applications ranging from machine translation and speech recognition to text analysis and natural language generation.

Finally, the study of linguistic diversity and language endangerment has become an increasingly important area of research in linguistics. With many languages and dialects at risk of disappearing, linguists have turned their attention to documenting and preserving endangered languages, as well as developing strategies for language revitalization and maintenance.

In conclusion, the study of linguistics has evolved over time to become an interdisciplinary field that spans a wide range of topics and approaches. From exploring the cognitive mechanisms underlying language use to documenting endangered languages and advocating for linguistic diversity, linguistics offers many exciting avenues for further research and discovery.

The study of linguistics has a long and rich history, dating back to ancient times. In this chapter, we will explore the major developments in linguistic doctrines from Aristotle to contrastive linguistics.

Aristotelian Linguistics

The Greek philosopher Aristotle (384-322 BCE) was one of the earliest thinkers to study language systematically. In his work "On Interpretation," he introduced the idea of a sentence as a combination of subject and predicate. He also developed a classification of parts of speech, including nouns, verbs, and conjunctions. Aristotle believed that language reflected the structure of reality and that understanding language was essential to understanding the world.

Medieval Grammar and Scholasticism

During the Middle Ages, grammar became a central focus of study, particularly in the field of scholasticism. Scholars such as St. Augustine and St. Thomas Aquinas developed sophisticated grammatical theories that were based on Aristotelian philosophy. They saw language as a reflection of the divine order of the universe and believed that the study of grammar was essential to understanding the Bible.

The Enlightenment and the Rise of Empiricism

In the 17th and 18th centuries, the Enlightenment brought a new focus on empirical observation and scientific method. This led to the development of the field of historical linguistics, which sought to understand how languages change over time. The philosopher John Locke argued that language was not innate but rather a product of experience, and this paved the way for the rise of the field of linguistics as a scientific discipline.

Structural Linguistics

In the early 20th century, the field of linguistics underwent a major shift with the development of structural linguistics. This approach, championed by Ferdinand de Saussure, argued that the structure of language was more important than its meaning. Structural linguistics emphasized the study of the phonology, morphology, and syntax of languages and sought to identify the underlying structures that were shared by all languages.

Generative Linguistics

In the 1950s, Noam Chomsky developed the field of generative linguistics, which emphasized the innate capacity of the human mind for language acquisition. Chomsky argued that language was not simply a matter of learning rules but rather was an innate ability that was hardwired into the human brain. Generative linguistics sought to identify the underlying structures and rules that governed language production and comprehension.

Contrastive Linguistics

Contrastive linguistics is a relatively recent development in the history of linguistic doctrines. It is concerned with the study of the similarities and differences between languages, with a particular focus on how these differences affect language learning and translation. Contrastive linguistics seeks to identify the similarities and differences between languages at all levels, from phonology and grammar to discourse and pragmatics.

Conclusion

In conclusion, the history of linguistic doctrines has been marked by a range of different approaches and perspectives. From Aristotle's early work on language to the rise of contrastive linguistics, linguists have sought to understand the nature of language and how it is acquired and used. Each new development has built on the work of previous scholars, creating a rich and diverse field of study that continues to evolve and expand.

Chapter 7 History of Linguistic Doctrines - From Aristotle to Functional Linguistics

In this chapter, we will explore the history of linguistic doctrines from Aristotle to functional linguistics. Functional linguistics is a relatively recent approach to language study that focuses on how language is used to achieve communication goals.

Aristotelian Linguistics

Aristotle (384-322 BCE) was one of the earliest scholars to study language systematically. He believed that language reflected the structure of reality and developed a classification of parts of speech that included nouns, verbs, and conjunctions. Aristotle's work on language influenced later scholars, including the medieval grammarians.

Medieval Grammar and Scholasticism

During the Middle Ages, grammar became a central focus of study, particularly in the field of scholasticism. Scholars such as St. Augustine and St. Thomas Aquinas developed sophisticated grammatical theories that were based on Aristotelian philosophy. They saw language as a reflection of the divine order of the universe and believed that the study of grammar was essential to understanding the Bible.

The Enlightenment and the Rise of Empiricism

In the 17th and 18th centuries, the Enlightenment brought a new focus on empirical observation and scientific method. This led to the development of the field of historical linguistics, which sought to understand how languages change over time. The philosopher John Locke argued that language was not innate but rather a product of experience, paving the way for the rise of the field of linguistics as a scientific discipline.

Structural Linguistics

In the early 20th century, the field of linguistics underwent a major shift with the development of structural linguistics. This approach, championed by Ferdinand de Saussure, argued that the structure of language was more important than its meaning. Structural linguistics emphasized the study of the phonology, morphology, and syntax of languages and sought to identify the underlying structures that were shared by all languages.

Generative Linguistics

In the 1950s, Noam Chomsky developed the field of generative linguistics, which emphasized the innate capacity of the human mind for language acquisition. Chomsky argued that language was not simply a matter of learning rules but rather was an innate ability that was hardwired into the human brain. Generative linguistics sought to identify the underlying structures and rules that governed language production and comprehension.

Functional Linguistics

Functional linguistics emerged in the 1970s as a response to the limitations of structural and generative linguistics. This approach emphasized the study of how language is used to achieve communication goals, rather than just the formal properties of language. Functional linguistics sees language as a social practice that is shaped by the communicative needs of the speakers and the cultural context in which they operate. It emphasizes the role of context in shaping language use and the importance of analyzing language in use, rather than just in isolation.

Conclusion

In conclusion, the history of linguistic doctrines has been marked by a range of different approaches and perspectives. From Aristotle's early work on language to the emergence of functional linguistics, linguists have sought to understand the nature of language and how it is acquired and used. Each new development has built on the work of previous scholars, creating a rich and diverse field of study that continues to evolve and expand. Functional linguistics is just one example of how linguistic theories can be revised and updated to reflect new discoveries and changing perspectives.

The history of linguistic doctrines from Aristotle to functional linguistics. Each period has contributed to the development of linguistic theories, with each approach building on the work of previous scholars.

Aristotle's work on language classification influenced later scholars, particularly the medieval grammarians who saw language as reflecting the divine order of the universe. During the Enlightenment, John Locke's philosophy challenged the notion of innate language, leading to the development of historical linguistics. The emergence of structural linguistics in the early 20th century shifted the focus to the formal properties of language, while generative linguistics emphasized the innate capacity for language acquisition.

Functional linguistics, which emerged in the 1970s, took a different approach. Instead of just studying the formal properties of language, functional linguistics focused on how language is used to achieve communication goals. It sees language as a social practice shaped by the communicative needs of speakers and their cultural context.

Overall, the history of linguistic doctrines demonstrates the evolution and diversity of linguistic theories. Each approach has contributed to a deeper understanding of language and its role in human communication. Functional linguistics is just one example of how linguistic theories can continue to evolve and be revised to reflect changing perspectives and new discoveries.

Throughout the history of linguistic doctrines, scholars have approached language from a variety of angles, each contributing to the development of linguistic theories. Aristotle's work on language classification established the groundwork for future grammatical analyses, while the medieval grammarians built on his work by seeing language as a reflection of the divine order of the universe.

During the Enlightenment, John Locke challenged the notion of innate language, leading to the development of historical linguistics, which sought to understand how languages change over time. The rise of structural linguistics in the early 20th century shifted the focus to the formal properties of language, emphasizing the study of phonology, morphology, and syntax to identify underlying structures shared by all languages.

In the 1950s, Noam Chomsky developed generative linguistics, which emphasized the innate capacity for language acquisition and sought to identify the underlying structures and rules that govern language production and comprehension. However, functional linguistics, which emerged in the 1970s, took a different approach. Instead of just studying the formal properties of language, functional linguistics focused on how language is used to achieve communication goals, emphasizing the importance of context in shaping language use and the social practice of language.

In summary, the history of linguistic doctrines highlights the diversity and evolution of linguistic theories. Each approach has built on the work of previous scholars, deepening our understanding of language and its role in human communication. As the field of linguistics continues to evolve, new perspectives and discoveries will likely lead to further revisions and updates to linguistic theories.

The study of language has a rich and complex history, with scholars from different periods and disciplines approaching language from various angles. Aristotle's work on language classification, for example, established the groundwork for future grammatical analyses, while the medieval grammarians built on his work by seeing language as a reflection of the divine order of the universe. These early linguistic theories were characterized by an emphasis on the structural properties of language and how they reflected larger philosophical and religious beliefs.

The Enlightenment period marked a shift in linguistic theories, with John Locke challenging the idea of innate language and leading to the development of historical linguistics. This approach sought to understand how languages change over time, and the role of socio-historical factors in shaping language use. In the early 20th century, structural linguistics emerged as a dominant approach, emphasizing the study of phonology, morphology, and syntax to identify underlying structures shared by all languages.

The 1950s saw the development of generative linguistics, which focused on the innate capacity for language acquisition and sought to identify the underlying structures and rules that govern language production and comprehension. However, this approach was criticized for its narrow focus on formal properties of language and its failure to account for the social and cultural context of language use.

In response, functional linguistics emerged in the 1970s, which took a more holistic approach to language. This approach emphasized the importance of context in shaping language use and the social practice of language. It viewed language as a tool for achieving communication goals, rather than just a set of formal structures to be analyzed in isolation.

Overall, the history of linguistic doctrines shows how linguistic theories have evolved and diversified over time, building on the work of previous scholars and deepening our understanding of language and its role in human communication. As linguistics continues to evolve, new discoveries and perspectives.

are likely to emerge, leading to further revisions and updates to linguistic theories. This dynamic process of theory-building reflects the complexity and richness of language as a human phenomenon, which cannot be fully understood from a single perspective or approach.

Furthermore, the history of linguistic doctrines highlights the interdisciplinary nature of linguistics, with scholars drawing on insights from philosophy, psychology, anthropology, sociology, and other fields to enrich their understanding of language. This interdisciplinary approach has enabled linguists to explore language from multiple angles, taking into account the diverse range of factors that shape language use and development.

In conclusion, the study of language has a long and diverse history, with each period contributing to the development of linguistic theories in different ways. From Aristotle to functional linguistics, each approach has built on the work of previous scholars, deepening our understanding of language and its role in human communication. As the field of linguistics continues to evolve, it will undoubtedly remain an exciting and dynamic area of research, revealing new insights and perspectives on language and its complex relationship with human thought and culture.

In addition to the interdisciplinary nature of linguistics, the history of linguistic doctrines also highlights the importance of considering language in its broader cultural and historical context. Language is not only a means of communication but also a reflection of social, cultural, and political dynamics. For instance, in the postcolonial era, linguists have highlighted how language policies and practices can be used to reinforce or challenge power imbalances between different groups.

Moreover, the study of language has increasingly incorporated insights from cognitive science, neuroscience, and artificial intelligence. These fields have shed new light on the cognitive processes underlying language production and comprehension, and on how language is represented and processed in the brain. This interdisciplinary approach has opened up new avenues for exploring the complex relationship between language, cognition, and culture.

In summary, the history of linguistic doctrines demonstrates the evolution and diversity of linguistic theories, highlighting the interdisciplinary and dynamic nature of the field. As linguistics continues to evolve, incorporating new perspectives and approaches, it will undoubtedly remain a rich and fascinating area of research, offering valuable insights into the complex relationship between language, culture, and cognition.

Chapter 6 History of Linguistic Doctrines - From Aristotle to Cognitive Linguistics

In this chapter, we will explore the history of linguistic doctrines from Aristotle to cognitive linguistics. Cognitive linguistics is a relatively new field of study that has gained popularity in recent years, and we will examine how it developed out of earlier linguistic theories.

The history of linguistic doctrines from Aristotle to cognitive linguistics highlights the evolution of linguistics as a field of study. Aristotle's work on language was influential in developing a classification of parts of speech that has continued to shape linguistic theory. In the Middle Ages, grammar became a central focus, and St. Augustine and St. Thomas Aquinas developed grammatical theories based on Aristotelian philosophy. During the Enlightenment, the field of historical linguistics emerged, emphasizing the study of how languages change over time. The rise of structural linguistics in the early 20th century shifted the focus to the structure of language rather than its meaning. Generative linguistics emerged in the 1950s, emphasizing the innate capacity of the human mind for language acquisition. Cognitive linguistics, which emerged in the 1970s, rejected the idea of language as an innate module of the mind and emphasized the role of cognitive processes in language acquisition and use.

In conclusion, the history of linguistic doctrines shows that linguistic theories and perspectives have evolved over time, influenced by changing intellectual and philosophical contexts. Each approach builds on the work of previous scholars and contributes to a rich and diverse field of study that continues to evolve and expand. By understanding the historical development of linguistic doctrines, scholars can better appreciate the complex nature of language and the many ways it shapes our understanding of the world.

Furthermore, the evolution of linguistic doctrines also highlights the interdisciplinary nature of linguistics. Throughout its history, linguistics has drawn on fields such as philosophy, psychology, anthropology, and computer science to develop new theories and approaches. This interdisciplinary approach has contributed to the richness of the field and allowed for new perspectives and insights.

Moreover, the history of linguistic doctrines also reveals the significance of cultural and social contexts in shaping linguistic theories. Theories of language have been influenced by societal beliefs and values, as well as the cultural practices and experiences of different communities. For instance, the focus on grammar during the Middle Ages was driven by the importance of religious texts, while the rise of historical linguistics in the Enlightenment was influenced by the growing interest in cultural and linguistic diversity.

Finally, the history of linguistic doctrines reminds us of the importance of critical reflection and revision in intellectual inquiry. As new discoveries and perspectives emerge, linguistic theories must be revised and updated to account for these changes. The emergence of cognitive linguistics, for example, was a response to the limitations of generative linguistics and reflected a shift in focus towards the role of cognitive processes in language acquisition and use.

In summary, the history of linguistic doctrines provides a fascinating journey through the development of linguistic theories over time. From Aristotle's early work to the emergence of cognitive linguistics, the field of linguistics has been shaped by a range of intellectual, cultural, and social contexts. By understanding this history, linguists can continue to develop new theories and perspectives that deepen our understanding of language and its role in shaping our world.

Linguistics, as a field, has always been open to cross-disciplinary exploration and has benefitted from the contributions of other fields in shaping its theories and approaches. This interdisciplinary approach has not only enriched the field but also facilitated a more comprehensive understanding of language and its role in shaping human life.

In addition to the interdisciplinary approach, cultural and social contexts have also been instrumental in shaping linguistic theories. For instance, the development of different linguistic theories can be linked to societal beliefs, cultural practices, and experiences of different communities. The cultural and social contexts, in turn, affect how language is learned, used, and perceived by individuals and communities.

Critical reflection and revision are also critical components of the evolution of linguistic doctrines. This process of critical inquiry requires a continuous revision of theories and approaches to incorporate new insights and discoveries that emerge from interdisciplinary exploration, cultural and social contexts, and scientific research. The development of cognitive linguistics, for example, emerged from the need to revise and update generative linguistics by emphasizing the role of cognitive processes in language acquisition and use.

In conclusion, the evolution of linguistic doctrines demonstrates the significance of interdisciplinary approaches, cultural and social contexts, and critical reflection and revision in shaping linguistic theories and perspectives. As linguistic research continues to evolve and expand, it is essential to appreciate the historical context in which linguistic theories emerged and how they have been shaped by a range of factors. Ultimately, a better understanding of the evolution of linguistic doctrines can help in developing new theories and approaches that contribute to a more profound comprehension of language and its role in human life.

Furthermore, the evolution of linguistic doctrines has also been influenced by advances in technology. The development of computer science and artificial intelligence has led to new approaches to language processing and understanding. Computational linguistics, for example, is a field that combines linguistics with computer science to develop algorithms and models for analyzing language data. This has led to significant advances in natural language processing, speech recognition, and machine translation, among other areas.

Moreover, linguistic theories have also been influenced by the study of language acquisition and development in children. This field of study, known as developmental psycholinguistics, has contributed to our understanding of how language is acquired and the cognitive processes involved in language development. Theories such as the social interactionist theory, which emphasizes the role of social interaction and context in language acquisition, have emerged from this field.

Finally, the evolution of linguistic doctrines has also been influenced by the study of language variation and change. Sociolinguistics, for example, is a field that examines how language varies across different social contexts, such as regional dialects, social class, and ethnicity. This has led to a better understanding of how language is used to convey social identity and how it reflects social hierarchies and power relations.

In summary, the evolution of linguistic doctrines has been shaped by a range of factors, including interdisciplinary approaches, cultural and social contexts, advances in technology, language acquisition and development in children, and language variation and change. By taking into account these diverse perspectives, linguistics has developed into a rich and dynamic field that continues to evolve and expand. As new insights and discoveries emerge, it is essential to continue to revise and update linguistic theories and approaches to deepen our understanding of language and its role.

The evolution of linguistic doctrines has been significantly impacted by the advancements in technology. The development of computer science and artificial intelligence has led to a new subfield in linguistics, computational linguistics. Computational linguistics has helped develop new approaches to language processing and understanding. The use of algorithms and models for analyzing language data has resulted in significant advancements in natural language processing, speech recognition, and machine translation.

In addition to technology, the study of language acquisition and development in children has also contributed to the evolution of linguistic doctrines. The field of developmental psycholinguistics has played a vital role in our understanding of how language is acquired and the cognitive processes involved in language development. Theories such as the social interactionist theory have emerged from this field, emphasizing the role of social interaction and context in language acquisition.

Furthermore, the study of language variation and change has also influenced linguistic theories. Sociolinguistics examines how language varies across different social contexts, such as regional dialects, social class, and ethnicity. This has led to a better understanding of how language is used to convey social identity and how it reflects social hierarchies and power relations.

Finally, it is essential to note that the evolution of linguistic doctrines has not been a linear process. The field has been subject to various intellectual movements and paradigms, including structuralism, generative grammar, and cognitive linguistics. Each paradigm has contributed to the development of linguistic theories and approaches.

In conclusion, the evolution of linguistic doctrines has been shaped by a range of factors, including interdisciplinary approaches, cultural and social contexts, technological advancements, language acquisition and development in children, and language variation and change. It is critical to continue to revise and update linguistic theories and approaches as new insights and discoveries emerge to deepen our understanding the concepts to language as a whole.

Aristotelian Linguistics

Aristotle (384-322 BCE) was one of the earliest scholars to study language systematically. He believed that language reflected the structure of reality and developed a classification of parts of speech that included nouns, verbs, and conjunctions. Aristotle's work on language influenced later scholars, including the medieval grammarians.

Medieval Grammar and Scholasticism

During the Middle Ages, grammar became a central focus of study, particularly in the field of scholasticism. Scholars such as St. Augustine and St. Thomas Aquinas developed sophisticated grammatical theories that were based on Aristotelian philosophy. They saw language as a reflection of the divine order of the universe and believed that the study of grammar was essential to understanding the Bible.

The Enlightenment and the Rise of Empiricism

In the 17th and 18th centuries, the Enlightenment brought a new focus on empirical observation and scientific method. This led to the development of the field of historical linguistics, which sought to understand how languages change over time. The philosopher John Locke argued that language was not innate but rather a product of experience, paving the way for the rise of the field of linguistics as a scientific discipline.

Structural Linguistics

In the early 20th century, the field of linguistics underwent a major shift with the development of structural linguistics. This approach, championed by Ferdinand de Saussure, argued that the structure of language was more important than its meaning. Structural linguistics emphasized the study of the phonology, morphology, and syntax of languages and sought to identify the underlying structures that were shared by all languages.

Generative Linguistics

In the 1950s, Noam Chomsky developed the field of generative linguistics, which emphasized the innate capacity of the human mind for language acquisition. Chomsky argued that language was not simply a matter of learning rules but rather was an innate ability that was hardwired into the human brain. Generative linguistics sought to identify the underlying structures and rules that governed language production and comprehension.

Cognitive Linguistics

Cognitive linguistics emerged in the 1970s as a response to the limitations of generative linguistics. Cognitive linguistics rejected the idea that language was an innate module of the mind and instead emphasized the role of cognitive processes in language acquisition and use. Cognitive linguistics sees language as a form of meaning-making that is shaped by human experience and cultural context. It emphasizes the importance of embodied cognition, which means that language is shaped by our experiences of the world through our bodies and senses.

Conclusion

In conclusion, the history of linguistic doctrines has been marked by a range of different approaches and perspectives. From Aristotle's early work on language to the emergence of cognitive linguistics, linguists have sought to understand the nature of language and how it is acquired and used. Each new development has built on the work of previous scholars, creating a rich and diverse field of study that continues to evolve and expand. Cognitive linguistics is just one example of how linguistic theories can be revised and updated to reflect new discoveries and changing perspectives.

Chapter 1 The Importance of Language

Language is a vital aspect of human communication, culture, and identity. It is through language that we convey our thoughts, emotions, and ideas to others. Without language, human society as we know it would not exist. Therefore, understanding the importance of language and the role of linguistics in studying it is crucial.

Language plays a significant role in shaping our perceptions of the world around us. It allows us to communicate with each other, express our cultural identity, and share knowledge. Language is also a tool for learning, as it enables us to understand and engage with new information.

Linguistics is the scientific study of language and its structure. The scope of linguistics encompasses the study of all aspects of language, including its history, structure, use, and acquisition. Linguistics is an interdisciplinary field that draws on various disciplines such as psychology, anthropology, computer science, and philosophy.

Linguistics helps us to understand the mechanisms underlying language use and acquisition. It provides insights into how we learn language, how we use language to communicate, and how language varies across cultures and social contexts. By studying language and linguistics, we can better understand the ways in which language influences our social interactions, cognitive development, and cultural identity.

In addition to its practical applications, such as language teaching and language technology development, linguistics also has broader societal implications. It can help to promote social justice by highlighting the role of language in perpetuating social inequalities. Linguistics also provides a means of preserving and celebrating cultural diversity by documenting and analyzing minority and endangered languages.

In conclusion, language is an essential aspect of human communication, culture, and identity. It is through language that we convey meaning, express our thoughts and emotions, and interact with others. Linguistics is a crucial tool for understanding the structure and function of language and its role in shaping human society. By continuing to study and explore language and linguistics, we can gain a deeper understanding of ourselves, others, and the world around us.

Language and linguistics are essential to human communication, culture, and identity. Language allows us to express our ideas, thoughts, and emotions, and without it, human society would not exist. Linguistics is the scientific study of language and its structure, encompassing all aspects of language, including its history, structure, use, and acquisition.

Language shapes our perceptions of the world and our interactions with others. It is a tool for learning and understanding new information and sharing knowledge. Linguistics helps us understand the underlying mechanisms of language use and acquisition, allowing us to better understand how language influences our cognitive development, social interactions, and cultural identity.

Furthermore, linguistics has practical applications in language teaching and language technology development. It can also promote social justice by highlighting the role of language in perpetuating social inequalities. Linguistics also provides a means of preserving and celebrating cultural diversity by documenting and analyzing minority and endangered languages.

In conclusion, language and linguistics are critical to human communication, culture, and identity. Through the study of language and linguistics, we can better understand ourselves, others, and the world around us. By recognizing the importance of language and the role of linguistics in studying it, we can continue to explore and expand our understanding of this fundamental aspect of human life.

Language and linguistics are essential aspects of human communication, culture, and identity. They play a significant role in shaping our perceptions of the world, allowing us to express our ideas, thoughts, and emotions, and interact with others. Without language, human society would not exist, and without linguistics, we would not understand the complexities of language.

Language is not just a tool for communication; it is a means of cultural expression and identity. It helps to define our individual and group identities and is a way of preserving and celebrating cultural diversity. Linguistics provides a framework for studying and understanding language in its many forms, including its history, structure, use, and acquisition.

The study of linguistics has numerous practical applications, from language teaching and translation to the development of language technology. It can also help to promote social justice by highlighting the role of language in perpetuating social inequalities. For example, language policies that promote one language over another can create barriers for minority communities. Linguistics can also provide a means of preserving and revitalizing endangered languages, which are critical to the cultural heritage of many communities around the world.

In conclusion, language and linguistics are fundamental to human communication, culture, and identity. By studying language and linguistics, we can better understand ourselves, others, and the world around us. It is essential to recognize the importance of language and the role of linguistics in studying it so that we can continue to explore and expand our understanding of this critical aspect of human life.

Chapter 2 The Linguistic Picture of the World

Chapter 2: The Linguistic Picture of the World

Language is an essential part of human culture and identity, and the diversity of languages across the world reflects the richness and complexity of human experience. In this chapter, we will explore the linguistic picture of the world, including the diversity of languages, linguistic families and language isolates, linguistic diversity, and endangerment.

The Diversity of Languages

There are an estimated 7,000 languages spoken in the world today, with varying degrees of use and vitality. Some languages are spoken by millions of people, while others are spoken by only a few hundred or even fewer. Language distribution is not evenly spread across the world, with some regions having more linguistic diversity than others.

Linguistic Families and Language Isolates

Linguistic families are groups of languages that are related to each other through a common ancestor language. Languages within the same family share similar features such as vocabulary, grammar, and phonetics. Examples of linguistic families include the Indo-European family, the Sino-Tibetan family, and the Afro-Asiatic family.

Language isolates, on the other hand, are languages that are not related to any other language. They exist as unique languages with no known linguistic relatives. Examples of language isolates include Basque, which is spoken in the Basque region of Spain and France, and Korean, which is spoken in North and South Korea.

Linguistic Diversity

Linguistic diversity refers to the range of languages spoken in a particular region or country. The degree of linguistic diversity varies across the world, with some regions having many languages while others have only a few. Linguistic diversity can be influenced by a range of factors such as geography, history, migration, and social factors.

Endangered Languages

Language endangerment refers to the risk of a language ceasing to be spoken in the future. This can occur due to a range of factors such as language shift, language suppression, and language loss. Endangered languages are those that are at risk of disappearing in the near future.

The current state of language endangerment is concerning, with many languages facing extinction. It is estimated that around 43% of the world's languages are endangered, with many of these being spoken by indigenous peoples.

Efforts to preserve endangered languages are underway, with many linguists and language activists working to document and revitalize endangered languages. Language revitalization programs can include language teaching, language documentation, and community language projects.

Conclusion

In conclusion, the linguistic picture of the world is complex and diverse, reflecting the richness and complexity of human culture and experience. The diversity of languages across the world is a testament to the unique perspectives and worldviews that different cultures and societies bring to the human experience. However, many languages are endangered, and efforts must be made to preserve and revitalize these languages to ensure their survival and continuation for future generations.

The English language is one of the most widely spoken languages in the world, with an estimated 1.5 billion speakers. However, the English language has not always been as we know it today. In this chapter, we will explore the history of the English language, from its earliest origins to its present-day form.

Old English

Old English, also known as Anglo-Saxon, was spoken in England from the 5th century until the 11th century. Old English was a Germanic language that was heavily influenced by Latin and Scandinavian languages. The earliest known Old English text is the poem Beowulf, which dates back to the 8th century. Old English had a complex system of grammar and a large vocabulary, with many words still in use today.

Middle English

Middle English was spoken in England from the 11th century until the late 15th century. Middle English was a period of great change for the English language, with the influence of French and Latin leading to many changes in grammar, vocabulary, and pronunciation. During this period, English was also heavily influenced by the printing press, which standardized spelling and helped to spread the language more widely.

Early Modern English

Early Modern English was spoken in England from the late 15th century until the mid-17th century. Early Modern English saw many changes in grammar, vocabulary, and pronunciation, with the language becoming more standardized and more closely resembling the English we know today. During this period, English also began to spread around the world, with colonization leading to the development of new varieties of English.

Modern English

Modern English is the form of English that is spoken today. Modern English is a global language, spoken by over 1.5 billion people around the world. Modern English has a standardized grammar and spelling system, and is constantly evolving, with new words and phrases being added to the language all the time.

Conclusion

In conclusion, the history of the English language is a long and complex one, with many influences shaping the language we know today. From its Germanic origins to its modern global form, the English language has undergone many changes throughout its history, with each period leaving its mark on the language. Understanding the history of the English language can help us to better appreciate the richness and diversity of this global language.

The linguistic picture of the world refers to the idea that language shapes our understanding of the world around us. According to this view, our perception of reality is mediated by language, and the way we think about and describe the world is influenced by the structure and vocabulary of the language(s) we use.

This perspective is based on the idea that language is not just a means of communication, but also a tool for thought. The words and structures of a language can shape our perceptions and ways of thinking about the world. For example, languages with a rich vocabulary for describing color may lead speakers to perceive and categorize colors differently from languages with a more limited vocabulary for color.

Linguistic relativity, also known as the Sapir-Whorf hypothesis, is a related idea that suggests that the structure of a language can affect the way its speakers perceive and think about the world. While there is ongoing debate about the extent to which language shapes thought, many linguists and cognitive scientists agree that language does have some influence on our perception and understanding of reality.

The linguistic picture of the world has important implications for fields such as cross-cultural communication and language learning. Understanding how language shapes our perception of reality can help us to better understand and communicate with people from different cultures and linguistic backgrounds.

Moreover, the linguistic picture of the world highlights the importance of studying languages and linguistics. By studying language and its relationship to thought and perception, we can gain a deeper understanding of how language shapes our understanding of the world and the ways in which different languages and cultures vary in their expression and interpretation of reality.

In conclusion, the linguistic picture of the world suggests that language shapes our perception and understanding of the world around us. By recognizing the influence of language on thought and perception, we can gain a deeper understanding of ourselves, others, and the world around us.

Studying language and linguistics can provide insights into the ways in which language influences our cognitive development, social interactions, and cultural identity. It can also help us to appreciate and value linguistic diversity and promote cross-cultural understanding.

By recognizing the linguistic picture of the world, we can approach communication and understanding with a more open and flexible mindset. We can recognize that different languages and cultures may have different ways of expressing and perceiving reality, and that these differences are not necessarily better or worse, but simply different.

Furthermore, understanding the linguistic picture of the world can be useful in practical applications such as language teaching and translation. It can help language learners to understand the cultural context and connotations of the words they are learning, and translators to convey meaning accurately between languages and cultures.

In summary, the linguistic picture of the world is an important perspective in understanding the role of language in shaping our perception and understanding of reality. By recognizing this influence, we can better appreciate linguistic diversity, promote cross-cultural understanding, and improve our communication and translation skills.

Studying language and linguistics can provide valuable insights into the ways in which language shapes our cognitive development, social interactions, and cultural identity. The linguistic picture of the world highlights the role of language in mediating our perception of reality, and understanding this perspective can promote a more open and flexible approach to communication and understanding.

By recognizing that different languages and cultures may have different ways of expressing and perceiving reality, we can approach cross-cultural communication with greater sensitivity and understanding. This is particularly important in an increasingly globalized world, where interactions between people from different linguistic and cultural backgrounds are becoming more frequent.

Moreover, understanding the linguistic picture of the world can have practical applications in fields such as language teaching and translation. Language learners can benefit from an understanding of the cultural context and connotations of the words they are learning, while translators can use their knowledge of the linguistic picture of the world to convey meaning accurately between languages and cultures.

Finally, studying language and linguistics can help us to appreciate and value linguistic diversity, which is an important aspect of cultural diversity. The world's linguistic diversity reflects the rich and varied ways in which different cultures express and perceive reality, and by recognizing the importance of this diversity, we can promote cross-cultural understanding and respect.

In conclusion, the linguistic picture of the world is a valuable perspective that highlights the important role of language in shaping our perception and understanding of reality. By recognizing this influence and studying language and linguistics, we can promote cross-cultural understanding, improve our communication skills, and appreciate the richness and diversity of human culture.

Well said! Studying language and linguistics can help us understand the intricacies of how language shapes our cognitive development, social interactions, and cultural identity. It can also promote a more sensitive and open-minded approach to cross-cultural communication, appreciation for linguistic diversity, and practical applications in language teaching and translation.

Moreover, an understanding of the linguistic picture of the world can have a significant impact on social and cultural issues. For example, it can shed light on the ways in which language can be used to perpetuate social inequalities, such as through the use of gendered language or the marginalization of minority languages. It can also help us recognize and challenge linguistic discrimination, such as the stigmatization of certain dialects or accents.

Overall, studying language and linguistics can provide valuable insights into the complex and dynamic relationship between language, culture, and society. It can help us understand the diverse ways in which people use language to express themselves, communicate, and make sense of the world around them. By embracing the linguistic picture of the world, we can promote greater understanding, respect, and appreciation for linguistics.

Chapter 3 Text Linguistics

Text linguistics is a branch of linguistics that focuses on the study of texts and their structure and organization. In this chapter, we will explore the definition and scope of text linguistics, discourse analysis, text types and functions, and text coherence and cohesion.

Definition and Scope of Text Linguistics

Text linguistics is concerned with the study of texts as meaningful units of language, rather than individual sentences or words. Texts are defined as communicative products that have a coherent and cohesive structure and serve a specific communicative purpose. Text linguistics investigates how texts are structured, how they are used to communicate meaning, and how they are interpreted by readers or listeners.

Discourse Analysis

Discourse analysis is a key aspect of text linguistics. It focuses on the analysis of larger units of language, such as conversations, speeches, and written texts. Discourse analysis aims to understand the social and cultural context in which texts are produced, the relationships between the speakers or writers and their audience, and the role of language in shaping social interaction and identity.

Text Types and Functions

Text types refer to the different forms that texts can take, such as narratives, descriptions, explanations, and arguments. Each text type has its own specific structure and language features, which are used to achieve a particular communicative function. For example, narratives are used to tell stories, while arguments are used to persuade and convince.

Text functions refer to the communicative purposes that texts serve. These purposes can range from providing information, expressing emotions, entertaining, or persuading. The functions of a text are closely related to its type and structure. For example, an informative text might have a clear and concise structure, while an emotive text might use language features such as imagery and figurative language to convey emotion.

Text Coherence and Cohesion

Text coherence and cohesion are two important concepts in text linguistics. Coherence refers to the logical and meaningful connections between different parts of a text. Cohesion, on the other hand, refers to the linguistic features that are used to link different parts of a text together. Cohesion can be achieved through the use of grammatical devices such as pronouns, conjunctions, and lexical repetition.

Coherence and cohesion are essential for ensuring that a text is easy to understand and that its communicative purpose is clear. A text that lacks coherence or cohesion may be confusing or difficult to follow.

Conclusion

In conclusion, text linguistics is a key area of study in linguistics that focuses on the structure and organization of texts and their communicative functions. Discourse analysis, text types and functions, and coherence and cohesion are all important aspects of text linguistics. Understanding these concepts is crucial for effective communication and for analyzing and interpreting written and spoken language in a range of contexts.

Text linguistics is a fascinating field of study that aims to understand how texts are structured, how they are used to communicate meaning, and how they are interpreted by readers or listeners. By examining the different types and functions of texts, text linguistics helps us to understand how language is used in social interaction and how it can shape our understanding of the world.

Discourse analysis is a crucial aspect of text linguistics that helps us to understand the social and cultural context in which texts are produced, as well as the relationships between the speakers or writers and their audience. By examining the language features and structures used in different types of texts, we can gain insights into the communicative purposes that they serve and the different ways in which language can be used to achieve these purposes.

Text coherence and cohesion are also important concepts in text linguistics, as they help to ensure that a text is easy to understand and that its communicative purpose is clear. By using linguistic features such as pronouns, conjunctions, and lexical repetition, we can create texts that are cohesive and coherent, and that effectively communicate their intended message.

In summary, text linguistics is a key area of study in linguistics that provides valuable insights into the structure and organization of texts, as well as the different ways in which language can be used to achieve specific communicative purposes. By understanding the concepts of discourse analysis, text types and functions, and coherence and cohesion, we can become more effective communicators and better able to analyze and interpret written and spoken language in a variety of contexts.

Text linguistics is a valuable area of study that provides insight into the structure and organization of texts, as well as their communicative functions. This branch of linguistics is concerned with understanding how texts are structured, used to communicate meaning, and interpreted by readers or listeners. Discourse analysis is a critical component of text linguistics, as it seeks to understand the social and cultural context in which texts are produced and the role of language in shaping social interaction and identity.

Text types and functions are another important aspect of text linguistics. Different text types have their own specific structures and language features, which are used to achieve a particular communicative function. The functions of a text can range from providing information to expressing emotions, entertaining, or persuading.

Coherence and cohesion are essential for ensuring that a text is easy to understand and that its communicative purpose is clear. Coherence refers to the logical and meaningful connections between different parts of a text, while cohesion refers to the linguistic features used to link different parts of a text together. Cohesion can be achieved through the use of grammatical devices such as pronouns, conjunctions, and lexical repetition.

In summary, text linguistics is a critical area of study in

linguistics that offers valuable insights into the structure and organization of texts and their communicative functions. Understanding the concepts of discourse analysis, text types and functions, and coherence and cohesion is essential for effective communication and for analyzing and interpreting written and spoken language in a range of contexts.

Furthermore, text linguistics can be applied to various fields, such as education, language teaching, and communication studies. In education, text linguistics can help teachers design and evaluate language curricula and materials. In language teaching, it can assist teachers in teaching students how to produce and understand different types of texts effectively. In communication studies, text linguistics can be used to analyze and interpret different types of discourse, such as political speeches, news articles, and social media posts.

Moreover, text linguistics can also be used in natural language processing and computational linguistics. These fields aim to develop algorithms and software that can understand and generate human language. By understanding how texts are structured and organized, natural language processing algorithms can be improved to better understand and produce texts.

Overall, text linguistics is a valuable area of study that has practical applications in various fields. It offers insight into the structure and organization of texts, as well as their communicative functions, and can be applied to improve language teaching, communication studies, and natural language processing.

In addition to its practical applications, text linguistics also has theoretical implications. It challenges traditional views of language as a collection of isolated words and sentences and instead emphasizes the importance of understanding language as a system of meaning-making. By focusing on texts as meaningful units of language, text linguistics offers a more comprehensive and holistic approach to the study of language and communication.

Text linguistics also recognizes the importance of context in shaping the meaning of a text. Discourse analysis, a key component of text linguistics, emphasizes the importance of understanding the social and cultural context in which a text is produced and the role of language in shaping social interaction and identity. This recognition of context is essential for understanding the nuances and complexities of language use and communication.

In conclusion, text linguistics is a dynamic and multi-faceted field of study that has both practical and theoretical applications. It offers valuable insights into the structure and organization of texts, their communicative functions, and the role of language in shaping social interaction and identity. By recognizing the importance of context and focusing on texts as meaningful units of language, text linguistics provides a comprehensive and holistic approach to the study of language and communication. Its applications in education, language teaching, communication studies, and natural language processing demonstrate its relevance and importance in various fields.

Chapter 4 Discourse Linguistics

Discourse linguistics is a branch of linguistics that focuses on the study of language in use, including conversations, speeches, and written texts. This chapter will explore the definition and scope of discourse linguistics, discourse markers and discourse connectives, speech acts and pragmatics, and critical discourse analysis.

Definition and Scope of Discourse Linguistics

Discourse linguistics is concerned with the analysis of language use in context. It seeks to understand how language is used to communicate meaning, convey social and cultural values, and shape relationships between speakers or writers and their audience. Discourse linguistics examines the structure and organization of discourse, as well as the linguistic and non-linguistic factors that influence its interpretation.

Discourse Markers and Discourse Connectives

Discourse markers and discourse connectives are important concepts in discourse linguistics. They are used to signal the relationship between different parts of a discourse and to guide the interpretation of its meaning. Discourse markers are words or phrases that signal a change in the direction of discourse, such as "however," "moreover," or "in addition." Discourse connectives, on the other hand, link different parts of a discourse and show their relationship, such as "because," "therefore," or "although."

Speech Acts and Pragmatics

Speech acts are another important area of study in discourse linguistics. Speech acts refer to the ways in which speakers or writers use language to perform actions, such as making a request, giving advice, or apologizing. Speech acts are closely related to pragmatics, which is the study of how context influences the interpretation of meaning. Pragmatics explores how speakers or writers use language to achieve their communicative goals, taking into account factors such as the social and cultural context in which the communication occurs.

Critical Discourse Analysis

Critical discourse analysis is a methodological approach to the study of discourse that focuses on the analysis of power relations and ideological positions. It seeks to understand how language is used to reproduce or challenge dominant social and cultural values, and how it can be used to empower or disempower individuals or groups. Critical discourse analysis examines the linguistic and non-linguistic features of discourse, as well as the social and cultural context in which it occurs.

Conclusion

In conclusion, discourse linguistics is a crucial area of study in linguistics that focuses on the analysis of language use in context. Discourse markers and discourse connectives, speech acts and pragmatics, and critical discourse analysis are all important aspects of discourse linguistics. Understanding these concepts is essential for effective communication and for analyzing and interpreting written and spoken language in a range of contexts.

Discourse linguistics is a branch of linguistics that focuses on language use in context, including conversations, speeches, and written texts. Its scope is vast, covering various aspects of language use that influence meaning and interpretation. Discourse linguistics aims to understand the structural and organizational patterns of discourse, the relationship between language and context, and how language use shapes social and cultural values.

Discourse markers and discourse connectives are important tools in discourse linguistics. Discourse markers signal changes in direction within a discourse and can be used to indicate speaker attitudes, emphasize points, or introduce new information. Discourse connectives link different parts of a discourse and show how they are related. These devices facilitate understanding of the discourse and enable the listener or reader to make connections between different parts of the text.

Speech acts and pragmatics are also essential areas of study in discourse linguistics. Speech acts refer to the ways in which language is used to perform actions, such as making a promise or issuing a command. Pragmatics, on the other hand, is concerned with the study of meaning in context. It explores how language use is influenced by the social and cultural context in which it occurs, as well as the communicative intentions of the speaker or writer. Pragmatics also looks at how conversational implicature, or implied meaning, is conveyed in discourse.

Critical discourse analysis is a critical approach to discourse linguistics that examines the role of language in shaping power relations and ideology. It investigates how discourse can be used to either reproduce or challenge dominant social and cultural values and how language use can impact individuals or groups. Critical discourse analysis is a methodological approach that emphasizes the importance of analyzing both linguistic and non-linguistic features of discourse, including the social and cultural context in which it occurs.

In conclusion, discourse linguistics is an essential area of study in linguistics that explores the use of language in context. Discourse markers and connectives, speech acts and pragmatics, and critical discourse analysis are all crucial aspects of discourse linguistics. Understanding these concepts is necessary for effective communication and for analyzing and interpreting written and spoken language in various contexts.

Chapter 8 The Emergence of Knowledge about Language Among Different Peoples

The study of language has a long and complex history, and its emergence among different peoples has varied greatly. In this chapter, we will explore the early accounts of language, the discovery of non-Indo-European languages, the study of language in colonial contexts, comparative linguistics and language reconstruction, and the emergence of linguistic anthropology.

Early Accounts of Language

The earliest accounts of language can be found in ancient texts, such as the Tower of Babel story in the Bible and the Greek philosopher Plato's Cratylus. These texts reflect a belief that language was divinely inspired and that it represented a fundamental aspect of human existence. In the Cratylus, Plato suggests that words have a natural connection to the objects they represent, which laid the foundation for later theories of the relationship between language and thought.

The Discovery of Non-Indo-European Languages

During the Age of Exploration, European explorers encountered a wide variety of non-Indo-European languages, such as Quechua in South America and Swahili in East Africa. These encounters led to a growing interest in the study of languages beyond the traditional European languages, and many linguists began to document and analyze these languages.

The Study of Language in Colonial Contexts

The study of language in colonial contexts was often intertwined with political and economic interests. Colonial powers sought to understand the languages of the peoples they were colonizing in order to facilitate communication and control. This led to the development of grammars and dictionaries of local languages, which were often produced by colonial officials or Christian missionaries. However, these accounts often reflected the biases and assumptions of the authors, and they did not always accurately reflect the language as it was used by native speakers.

Comparative Linguistics and Language Reconstruction

The development of comparative linguistics in the 19th century revolutionized the study of language by providing a scientific framework for the comparison of languages. This approach involved comparing the vocabulary and grammar of different languages in order to identify similarities and differences, which allowed linguists to reconstruct the ancestral language from which they all descended. This led to the development of the Proto-Indo-European language, which is the hypothetical common ancestor of all Indo-European languages.

Linguistic Anthropology

The emergence of linguistic anthropology in the 20th century marked a shift in the study of language from a purely linguistic perspective to a more social and cultural one. Linguistic anthropologists sought to understand the role of language in shaping social relations, cultural practices, and identity formation. This approach emphasized the importance of context in shaping language use and the ways in which language both reflected and influenced cultural practices.

In conclusion, the emergence of knowledge about language among different peoples has been shaped by a variety of historical and cultural factors. From early accounts of language to the development of comparative linguistics and linguistic anthropology, the study of language has evolved over time, deepening our understanding of its role in human communication and culture.

The study of language has a long and complex history, and its emergence among different peoples has varied greatly. In this chapter, we will explore the early accounts of language, the discovery of non-Indo-European languages, the study of language in colonial contexts, comparative linguistics and language reconstruction, and the emergence of linguistic anthropology.

Early Accounts of Language

The earliest accounts of language can be found in ancient texts, such as the Tower of Babel story in the Bible and the Greek philosopher Plato's Cratylus. These texts reflect a belief that language was divinely inspired and that it represented a fundamental aspect of human existence. In the Cratylus, Plato suggests that words have a natural connection to the objects they represent, which laid the foundation for later theories of the relationship between language and thought.

The Discovery of Non-Indo-European Languages

During the Age of Exploration, European explorers encountered a wide variety of non-Indo-European languages, such as Quechua in South America and Swahili in East Africa. These encounters led to a growing interest in the study of languages beyond the traditional European languages, and many linguists began to document and analyze these languages.

The Study of Language in Colonial Contexts

The study of language in colonial contexts was often intertwined with political and economic interests. Colonial powers sought to understand the languages of the peoples they were colonizing in order to facilitate communication and control. This led to the development of grammars and dictionaries of local languages, which were often produced by colonial officials or Christian missionaries. However, these accounts often reflected the biases and assumptions of the authors, and they did not always accurately reflect the language as it was used by native speakers.

Comparative Linguistics and Language Reconstruction

The development of comparative linguistics in the 19th century revolutionized the study of language by providing a scientific framework for the comparison of languages. This approach involved comparing the vocabulary and grammar of different languages in order to identify similarities and differences, which allowed linguists to reconstruct the ancestral language from which they all descended. This led to the development of the Proto-Indo-European language, which is the hypothetical common ancestor of all Indo-European languages.

Linguistic Anthropology

The emergence of linguistic anthropology in the 20th century marked a shift in the study of language from a purely linguistic perspective to a more social and cultural one. Linguistic anthropologists sought to understand the role of language in shaping social relations, cultural practices, and identity formation. This approach emphasized the importance of context in shaping language use and the ways in which language both reflected and influenced cultural practices.

In conclusion, the emergence of knowledge about language among different peoples has been shaped by a variety of historical and cultural factors. From early accounts of language to the development of comparative linguistics and linguistic anthropology.

the study of language has been a dynamic and ever-evolving field of study. One area of research that has gained prominence in recent years is the study of multilingualism and language contact.

Multilingualism refers to the use of two or more languages in daily life, whether by individuals, communities, or entire countries. This phenomenon is increasingly common in today's globalized world, and it presents unique challenges and opportunities for language researchers. For example, linguists are interested in understanding how multilingual speakers switch between languages, how they use different languages for different purposes, and how they navigate complex linguistic and cultural identities.

Language contact refers to the situation where two or more languages come into contact and interact with each other. This can happen through migration, colonization, trade, or other forms of interaction. Language contact can lead to the creation of new hybrid languages, such as creoles or pidgins, or it can result in the borrowing of words and grammatical structures from one language into another.

The study of multilingualism and language contact is important for several reasons. First, it provides insights into how languages change and evolve over time, as well as how they adapt to new social and cultural contexts. Second, it helps to shed light on issues related to language maintenance and language loss, particularly in situations where minority languages are in danger of disappearing. Finally, it has important implications for education and language policy, as it highlights the importance of valuing and supporting linguistic diversity.

In conclusion, the study of language is a rich and multifaceted field, encompassing a wide range of topics and approaches. From early philosophical musings on the nature of language to contemporary research on multilingualism and language contact, the study of language has played a central role in our understanding of what it means to be human. As we continue to explore the complexities of language and communication, we can expect new insights and discoveries that will deepen our appreciation for the role that language plays in our lives.

Chapter 9 Conclusion

As we reflect on the fascinating journey through the history, theories, and applications of linguistics, it is clear that the study of language is essential for understanding human communication, cognition, and culture. From the origins of language to the intricacies of its structure and use, we have explored the many aspects of linguistics and its interdisciplinary connections.

One of the main takeaways from this book is the importance of linguistic diversity and the need to preserve endangered languages. Languages are not just means of communication, but also carriers of cultural heritage and identity. Therefore, efforts to document, revitalize, and maintain endangered languages are crucial for promoting linguistic and cultural diversity.

Another significant theme that emerged from this book is the ethical considerations that arise when conducting linguistic research. As linguists, we need to be aware of the power dynamics that exist between researchers and research participants, especially when working with marginalized communities. We need to prioritize informed consent and representation to ensure that our work does not perpetuate existing inequalities and biases.

Looking towards the future, there are many exciting directions for linguistics research. The study of language evolution and the relationship between language and the brain can provide insights into the development of human cognition and culture. Additionally, the application of linguistics to real-world problems can inform language policy and promote equitable and inclusive language practices.

Linguistic knowledge has far-reaching implications for society and culture, and it is crucial for linguists and language professionals to promote understanding and respect across linguistic and cultural boundaries. We need to be aware of the potential social and cultural implications of our work and work towards promoting equitable and inclusive language practices.

In conclusion, this book has provided a comprehensive and accessible introduction to the many facets of linguistics. As we continue to explore this fascinating field, we can hope to gain a deeper understanding of human communication, cognition, culture, and society.

We have also seen that linguistics is an interdisciplinary field, with connections to psychology, anthropology, neuroscience, philosophy, computer science, and many other disciplines. These interdisciplinary connections allow for a more holistic understanding of language and its role in human behavior and society.

One of the most significant challenges in linguistics is the issue of language universals and variation. While there are many commonalities across languages, there are also significant differences in terms of syntax, morphology, phonology, and semantics. Understanding the nature and extent of these variations is crucial for understanding language and its role in human communication.

Another challenge in linguistics is the study of language acquisition. While we have made significant progress in understanding how children learn language, many questions remain about the cognitive processes that underlie language acquisition. These questions are particularly important for understanding language development in multilingual and multicultural contexts.

Finally, as linguistics continues to evolve, there is a growing need for linguists to engage with broader societal issues. Language policy, language education, and language rights are all areas where linguistic expertise can inform policy decisions and promote equitable and inclusive language practices.

In summary, the study of linguistics is a fascinating and dynamic field that has much to offer in terms of understanding language, cognition, culture, and society. By promoting linguistic diversity, prioritizing ethical considerations.

in research, and engaging with interdisciplinary perspectives, linguistics can continue to make valuable contributions to our understanding of human communication and behavior. The challenges of language universals and variation, language acquisition, and societal issues provide exciting avenues for future research and practical applications.

As linguists, it is essential to be mindful of the impact of our work and prioritize ethical considerations. This includes being aware of potential biases and power dynamics in research, as well as promoting equitable and inclusive language practices in society. By doing so, we can help to bridge linguistic and cultural boundaries, promote understanding, and contribute to a more just and equitable world.

In addition to the challenges and opportunities discussed in this book, there are many emerging areas of research that offer exciting possibilities for the future of linguistics. One such area is the study of linguistic typology, which seeks to identify patterns in the structures of languages and the ways in which they vary across different cultures and regions. Through the use of computational methods and large-scale data analysis, linguists can now identify linguistic features that are common to certain language families or regions, as well as those that are unique to particular languages.

Another area of growing interest is the study of language evolution. By analyzing the fossil record and genetic data, as well as studying the communication patterns of non-human animals, linguists and evolutionary biologists are gaining insights into how language might have evolved in humans. This research is shedding light on the cognitive and social factors that may have contributed to the development of language, as well as the evolutionary pressures that may have shaped its structure and use.

Finally, the study of language in context is also becoming increasingly important. As society becomes more globalized and multicultural, understanding how language is used in different social and cultural contexts is critical for effective communication and for promoting social and linguistic equality. This includes studying the ways in which language is used in different professional, educational, and political settings, as well as the ways in which language is used to negotiate power and identity.

In conclusion, linguistics is a complex and fascinating field that offers many avenues for future research and practical applications. By embracing interdisciplinary perspectives, promoting ethical considerations, and engaging with emerging areas of research, linguists can continue to make valuable contributions to our understanding of human communication and behavior. Ultimately, these efforts can help to promote greater understanding, respect, and equality across linguistic and cultural boundaries.

This overview highlights some emerging areas of research in the field of linguistics that offer exciting possibilities for the future. One such area is linguistic typology, which aims to identify patterns in the structures of languages and their variations across cultures and regions. Computational methods and large-scale data analysis have enabled linguists to identify linguistic features common to certain language families or regions, as well as those unique to particular languages.

The study of language evolution is another area of growing interest, with researchers using fossil records, genetic data, and observations of non-human animal communication patterns to gain insights into how language evolved in humans. This research is shedding light on the cognitive and social factors that may have contributed to language development, as well as the evolutionary pressures that may have shaped its structure and use.

Finally, the study of language in context is becoming increasingly important in a globalized and multicultural society. Understanding how language is used in different social and cultural contexts is critical for effective communication and for promoting social and linguistic equality. This includes studying language use in various professional, educational, and political settings, as well as how language is used to negotiate power and identity.

As linguistics continues to evolve and embrace interdisciplinary perspectives, promote ethical considerations, and engage with emerging areas of research, it can continue to make valuable contributions to our understanding of human communication and behavior. Ultimately, these efforts can help to promote greater understanding, respect, and equality across linguistic and cultural boundaries.

As we come to the end of this book, we can reflect on the fascinating journey we have taken through the history, theories, and applications of linguistics. In this final chapter, we will summarize the main points of the book, discuss potential future directions for linguistics research, and explore the implications of linguistic knowledge for society and culture.

Summary of the Book We began our journey by exploring the origins and development of human language, discussing its complexity and universality across cultures. We then delved into the different components of language, including phonetics, phonology, morphology, syntax, and semantics, and how they interact to produce meaningful communication. We also examined how language is acquired, processed, and used by individuals and communities, and how it can vary across dialects and languages.

We then explored the many applications of linguistics, including language teaching, speech therapy, forensic linguistics, and machine translation. We also discussed the role of linguistics in fields such as psychology, anthropology, neuroscience, and philosophy, and how it can contribute to a deeper understanding of human cognition, culture, and social interaction.

Throughout the book, we highlighted the importance of linguistic diversity and the need to preserve endangered languages. We also emphasized the ethical considerations that arise when conducting linguistic research, such as issues of representation, power, and informed consent.

Future Directions in Linguistics Research As linguistics continues to evolve, there are many exciting avenues for future research. One promising area is the study of language evolution, which seeks to understand how and why human language has developed over time. This includes investigating the origins of language, the relationship between language and brain structure, and the ways in which language can change and diversify over generations.

Another area of interest is the study of language processing in the brain, using techniques such as neuroimaging and neurolinguistics. This research can shed light on the neural mechanisms that underlie language comprehension and production, as well as the relationship between language and other cognitive processes such as memory and attention.

Finally, there is growing interest in the application of linguistics to real-world problems, such as language policy, multilingual education, and language documentation. Linguistic research can help inform policy decisions and promote the maintenance and revitalization of endangered languages.

Implications of Linguistic Knowledge for Society and Culture Linguistic knowledge has far-reaching implications for society and culture. It can promote understanding and respect across linguistic and cultural boundaries, as well as facilitate communication and cooperation in diverse contexts. It can also contribute to the preservation of cultural heritage and the empowerment of marginalized communities.

However, linguistic knowledge can also be used to perpetuate inequality and discrimination. For example, language policies that promote only one dominant language can marginalize speakers of other languages and erode linguistic diversity. Similarly, linguistic stereotypes and biases can lead to prejudice and discrimination based on language use and accent.

Therefore, it is crucial for linguists and language professionals to be aware of the potential social and cultural implications of their work and to promote equitable and inclusive language practices.

In conclusion, the study of linguistics is a dynamic and interdisciplinary field that has much to offer in terms of understanding language, cognition, culture, and society. It is our hope that this book has provided a comprehensive and accessible introduction to the many facets of linguistics and has inspired readers to explore this fascinating field further.

Glossary

Language is a vital aspect of human communication, culture, and identity. It is the primary tool through which we convey meaning, express our thoughts and emotions, and interact with others. Without language, human society as we know it would not exist. Therefore, it is essential to understand the importance of language and the scope of linguistics in studying it.

This chapter will provide an overview of the importance of language, the scope of linguistics, and a brief historical overview of linguistics. Additionally, it will give an overview of the book.

The Importance of Language

Language is the fundamental means of communication among humans. It enables us to express our ideas, thoughts, and emotions to others. Language is not just a tool for communication, but it also shapes the way we view and understand the world around us. Language is a significant part of our identity, culture, and heritage.

The ability to use language is unique to humans and sets us apart from other animals. We can learn and use multiple languages, and each language reflects the culture and society in which it is used. Language also plays a crucial role in our cognitive development, shaping how we think and perceive the world.

The Scope of Linguistics

Linguistics is the scientific study of language and its structure, including the sounds, words, grammar, and meaning of language. The scope of linguistics encompasses the study of all aspects of language, including its history, structure, use, and acquisition.

Linguistics is an interdisciplinary field that draws on various disciplines such as psychology, anthropology, computer science, and philosophy. Linguists study language at different levels of analysis, including the phonetic, phonological, morphological, syntactic, and semantic levels.

Historical Overview of Linguistics

The study of language has a long and rich history that dates back to ancient times. Some of the earliest recorded discussions of language are found in the works of ancient Greek philosophers such as Plato and Aristotle. However, it was not until the 19th century that linguistics emerged as a formal academic discipline.

One of the key figures in the development of modern linguistics was Ferdinand de Saussure, a Swiss linguist who is considered the father of modern linguistics. Saussure introduced the idea that language is a system of signs that can be studied independently of their meaning.

Another important figure in linguistics was Noam Chomsky, who developed the theory of generative grammar, which proposes that language is an innate human capacity. Chomsky's work had a significant impact on the field of linguistics and influenced the study of language acquisition, language variation, and language change.

Overview of the Book

Exploring Linguistics From the Origins of Language to Modern Theories and Applications

This book aims to provide an in-depth exploration of various topics in linguistics, including the map of world languages, text linguistics, discourse linguistics, the history of linguistic doctrines, and the emergence of knowledge about language among different peoples.

In chapter 2, we will explore the linguistic picture of the world, including the diversity of languages, linguistic families and language isolates, linguistic diversity, and endangerment.

Chapter 3 will focus on text linguistics, including the definition and scope of text linguistics, discourse analysis, text types and functions, and text coherence and cohesion.

Chapter 4 will delve into discourse linguistics, including the definition and scope of discourse linguistics, discourse markers and connectives, speech acts and pragmatics, and critical discourse analysis.

Chapters 5, 6, and 7 will examine the history of linguistic doctrines, from Aristotle to contrastive linguistics, cognitive linguistics, and functional linguistics, respectively. Chapter 8 will discuss the emergence of knowledge about language among different peoples, including early accounts of language, the discovery of non-Indo-European languages, the study of the languages.

Chapter 9: Conclusion

Summary of the Book
Future Directions in Linguistics Research
Implications of Linguistic Knowledge for Society and Culture.

9 789356 677609